THE BAD LUCK PLAY

JANET LORIMER

SADDLEBACK
EDUCATIONAL PUBLISHING

QUICKREADS

SERIES 1

- Black Widow Beauty
- Danger on Ice
- Empty Eyes
- The Experiment
- The Kula'i Street Knights
- The Mystery Quilt
- No Way to Run
- The Ritual
- The 75-Cent Son
- The Very Bad Dream

SERIES 2

- The Accuser
- Ben Cody's Treasure
- Blackout
- The Eye of the Hurricane
- The House on the Hill
- Look to the Light
- Ring of Fear
- The Tiger Lily Code
- Tug-of-War
- The White Room

SERIES 3

- **The Bad Luck Play**
- Breaking Point
- Death Grip
- Fat Boy
- No Exit
- No Place Like Home
- The Plot
- Something Dreadful Down Below
- Sounds of Terror
- The Woman Who Loved a Ghost

SERIES 4

- The Barge Ghost
- Beasts
- Blood and Basketball
- Bus 99
- The Dark Lady
- Dimes to Dollars
- Read My Lips
- Ruby's Terrible Secret
- Student Bodies
- Tough Girl

SADDLEBACK
EDUCATIONAL PUBLISHING
www.sdlback.com

ISBN-13: 978-1-61651-198-2
ISBN-10: 1-61651-198-2
eBook: 978-1-60291-920-4

Printed in Guangzhou, China
0511/05-27-11

15 14 13 12 11 2 3 4 5 6

■ ■ ■

"*By the pricking of my thumbs, something wicked this way comes!*" Nick Finney paused and then grinned at his audience. "Anyone recognize that line?"

The hands of half a dozen high school students shot up. Nick glanced at the adults scattered about the room.

Nick was the new drama director at Cold Forks High School. He expected his students to recognize the line from a play they were studying. He wasn't so sure about the adults, though. They were members of a local little theater group. Right now they looked baffled.

One student waved his arm excitedly,

begging Nick to call on him. Nick was disappointed in the adults. They sat in their chairs as still as statues.

"Don't *any* of you recognize that line?" Nick asked the adults. "It's from Shakespeare's play *Macbeth.*"

In the front row, Joe Collier—the local newspaper publisher—shifted uneasily in his chair. "Some of us recognized the line, Nick. We know what play it's from. We just don't like it."

Nick studied Joe in surprise. "It's one of Shakespeare's greatest tragedies. How can anyone *not* like *Macbeth?*" When no one answered, Nick went on. "I hope you can learn to like it, Joe. My students are studying *Macbeth* this semester. So that's the play I want to direct for your little theater group!"

In the back row, Gloria Valdez stood up. She was a local businessperson who owned several stores in town. "Nick, we don't want to make life hard for you," she said with a nervous smile. "We just think it would be better if we put on a comedy or a musical.

Or maybe—"

Other people began throwing out ideas. Nick shook his head. "It will be better for all of us if we do *Macbeth,"* he insisted. "Then I can bring my students into the production. I've staged this play in other places, and everyone really liked it. It's a great story, filled with greed, betrayal, murder, ghosts—"

Harry Hardwick, the local bank president, stood up. *"Macbeth* is a bad luck play," he said flatly.

■ ■ ■

Nick was amazed. "Harry, are you kidding me? Are you folks really *that* superstitious?" he exclaimed.

Harry turned red and looked away.

Nick noticed that his students seemed puzzled. "Maybe I'd better explain," Nick told them. "There's a legend that Shakespeare wanted to make a big impression on the King of England, James I. So he included a real witch's curse in *Macbeth.* As a result, the play supposedly brings bad luck to the actors.

Even to this day, a lot of actors won't say the name of the play out loud. They refer to it as 'that Scottish play' or 'the cursed play.'"

Nick saw several students glance nervously at each other. He grinned. "Give me a break! You don't believe that old rubbish, do you?"

"What *kind* of bad luck?" asked Steve, a red-haired high school senior.

Nick laughed. "Sometimes actors have had accidents. But—" He paused, looking at each student in turn. Several of the faces looked worried. "Come on, you guys! Accidents happen all the time. There have been accidents in other shows. No one calls *them* bad luck plays."

Steve looked relieved. "So it's not *really* bad luck?"

"Only if you believe it is," Nick said. He stood up and stretched. "Okay, people, it's late. Let's wrap it up now so my students can go home and get to bed. I don't want to see any of them falling asleep in drama class tomorrow!"

The students laughed.

The adults didn't crack a smile. "Is your mind made up, Nick?" Gloria asked. "Is it *Macbeth* or nothing?"

Nick nodded. "I'm afraid so, Gloria. Of course, I'd understand if you guys decide to get someone else to direct your play—" He shrugged.

Several of the adults looked unhappy. "I guess we'll have to talk this over among ourselves," Joe said. "We'll get back to you, Nick."

Nick watched as everyone filed out of the classroom. "I wonder what's really going on here," he thought.

■ ■ ■

He didn't have to wait long to find out. The next morning, before class started, Nick got a phone call from Gloria. "This is your first year in Cold Forks," she said. "I'm not sure you know about the town's history with *Macbeth.*"

"History?" Nick asked.

"Five years ago, the little theater group actually staged *Macbeth,"* Gloria said. "It was a disaster from start to finish. I know you think we're just superstitious—but it's more than that."

Nick frowned. "What happened?"

"Right from the start there were accidents. It sounds crazy, but it's true."

Nick sighed. "Accidents happen. That's what I told my students last night. Come on, Gloria—"

"The theater caught fire," Gloria cut in. "It was during dress rehearsal, the night before we opened. Luckily, everyone got out in time. But that's why some of us don't want to do *Macbeth."*

Nick was silent for a moment. Then he said, "I can see why you'd be upset. But no one was hurt, and no one died. We have to show the kids that we don't believe in that superstitious nonsense. I'm not changing my mind, Gloria. It's *Macbeth* or nothing."

"You're making a big mistake, Nick!" Gloria snapped. Now Nick could hear the anger in her voice. *"Huge!"* She slammed down the receiver.

Nick figured he'd soon get another call—from Harry. Harry Hardwick was the president of the theater group. Nick was pretty sure he'd call to say they were looking for another director. But before the end of the week, Harry called to say that the group had agreed.

"We voted," Harry told Nick. "All the newcomers want to do *Macbeth*. They outnumber those of us who remember the fire. We still think it's foolish to put on a bad luck play."

"Give it a chance, Harry. It's time you all put that superstitious nonsense behind you," Nick said. "I promise—the community will *love* this production!"

■ ■ ■

"Double, double toil and trouble. Fire burn and cauldron bubble."

Nick stopped quoting. Considering the history of the Cold Forks theater fire, that line from *Macbeth* suddenly seemed to be in bad taste.

"Sorry," Nick mumbled as he glanced sideways at his three companions. Joe, Gloria, and Harry stared at him.

Then all four of them turned to study the boarded-up theater.

"This building should have been torn down after the fire," Gloria said crossly. "It's a disaster. I don't know why you want to go inside, Nick. We can't use it."

"It looks pretty good from the outside," Nick said, "and there's plenty of parking. I bet this theater can be restored."

"How many times do we have to tell you—the building is *unsafe!"* Harry said gruffly. He yanked out his handkerchief and wiped his forehead. He suddenly seemed very nervous.

"I guess I need to see it for myself," Nick said. "People say that the theater was fairly new at the time of the fire." Nobody commented, so Nick went on. "From the fire marshal's report it didn't seem that the structure was damaged too badly."

Gloria shivered. "I haven't been in the theater since that terrible night five years ago," Gloria said. "I'm not sure I want to go in now."

"Why don't you wait out here then," Nick suggested. He was getting tired of Gloria dragging her feet. "I don't mind going in by myself. Harry, do you have the keys?"

Harry unlocked the big padlock on the double doors. Nick checked his flashlight and then led the way inside. Joe and Harry followed right behind. The door slammed after them.

Maybe it was just his imagination, but Nick thought he could still smell smoke. He shone his light around the lobby. Aside from dust and spider webs, the room looked okay.

Nick moved from the lobby into the theater itself. As he examined the walls and ceiling, he was surprised to see very little smoke and water damage. He climbed on stage. Some of the old scenery was still stacked against the back wall. "Just where did the fire start?" he asked.

"In the prop room," Joe answered. Then the newspaperman led the way to the rear of the theater. Now Nick could see that this part of the building really was badly damaged. The prop room and dressing rooms were a charred mess.

"I wonder what it would cost to repair the theater," Nick said. He thought he heard Joe's sharp intake of breath.

"Too much money," Harry said quickly. "And there's no time. The play has to be ready for the tourists this summer. If we're lucky, it could be a good source of income for the town."

"Not without a theater," Nick said. "Where did you plan to stage this play?"

He saw Joe and Harry exchange glances. "At the high school," Joe said.

Nick shook his head. "That theater is way too small, Harry! It won't support a play like *Macbeth*. Besides—tourists expect a more professional setting than a high school auditorium."

"That's another good reason for doing a

different play," Harry said.

Nick didn't reply—but he suddenly had an idea about how to get the theater restored.

■ ■ ■

A week later, Nick attended the town council meeting at City Hall. When he walked into the meeting room, he saw Gloria, Joe, and Harry sitting at the back of the room. They seemed shocked to see him there. He smiled and waved—but he walked down the aisle and sat in the middle seat of the front row.

Nick raised his hand when the chairman asked if there was any new business. He quickly detailed his plan for repairing the old theater. "I have facts and figures," Nick said. "The theater was insured—but not for much. That's one reason it was never repaired. I'm hoping that some of the businesspeople in town will donate materials. And maybe we can get volunteers to do most of the work. That will cut down on the cost."

He paused to let his words sink in. Then

he said, "One more thing. That boarded-up theater is right in the center of town. It's an eyesore, wouldn't you say?" Several council members nodded. "There are businesses on each side," Nick went on. "The bank, for example, is right next door to the theater. And one of Gloria's shops is on the other side."

More people nodded. But their faces looked uncertain. Nick knew they were wondering what he was leading up to.

"Fixing up the theater," Nick said, "would help the town in more ways than one. It would make that shopping area much more attractive, for example. And a spruced-up appearance would bring in a lot more customers."

Nick could see that he had everyone's attention. People were getting excited. After a brief discussion, the council voted to restore the old theater.

Nick glanced at Joe, Harry, and Gloria. Their looks of anger surprised him. "I don't get it," Nick thought. "Those are the very people who stand to benefit the most!"

■ ■ ■

"Methought I heard a voice cry, 'Sleep no more! Macbeth does murder sleep.' "

"Mr. Finney, what does 'methought' mean?" Steve asked.

Nick smiled. "It means 'I thought,'" he explained. He and a small group of students were sitting backstage, going through one of the scenes. Onstage, several adult cast members were practicing their lines.

"Remember, this play was written about 400 years ago," Nick said. "In Shakespeare's time people didn't talk the way we talk today. I'll bet if Shakespeare heard you guys talking, he wouldn't understand *you,* either!"

The very idea made the students laugh. Nick acknowledged that the unfamiliar language could make Shakespeare's plays hard to read. "But when people actually see a play acted out," Nick added, "the language makes a lot more sense."

Nick went on to explain the rest of the quotation. In the story, he said, Macbeth had murdered his king. The shame of his evil deed kept him from getting a good night's rest. "He feels guilty. Can any of you relate to that?" Nick asked with a twinkle in his eye.

■ ■ ■

In the first few weeks after the town council meeting, everything went well. The community adopted the restoration of the theater as its main project. Every weekend, volunteers poured in to help with the repairs.

Meantime, Nick scheduled tryouts. He was surprised when Gloria tried out for the part of Lady Macbeth. "I thought you hated this play," he said.

She smiled coldly. "We have to put superstition behind us, remember?"

She climbed onstage and began reading from the script. Nick was amazed. Gloria was the *perfect* Lady Macbeth! She sounded cold, cruel, and greedy. "I wonder if that's what she's *really* like," Nick thought.

Nick was amused when Joe and Harry also tried out for parts in the play. What a surprise! The three people who claimed to be so afraid of *Macbeth* had gotten involved after all.

After Nick chose the cast, he looked for people to work on the crew. He needed stagehands, lighting technicians, and even more people to find props and sew the costumes.

Day by day, the restoration work was progressing well. Volunteers had already cleaned up the lobby. Now the walls sparkled with fresh paint, and the plush carpet had been cleaned.

Fresh paint also covered up the smoke and water stains in the theater itself. The seats had been re-covered with red brocade. The scorched stage curtains had been replaced with new curtains of gold-colored velvet.

The volunteers were about to start tearing down the badly burned rooms at the back. This would be the noisiest part of the restoration. Nick hoped the sounds of sawing and hammering wouldn't disturb the actors too much.

■ ■ ■

It was at that point that all the trouble started.

About midnight, the police chief phoned Nick at home. The ringing phone awoke him from a sound sleep.

"I think you better get down to the theater," the chief said. "I'm afraid there's been some vandalism."

"What?" Nick cried. Suddenly, he was fully awake.

"It looks like vandals spray-painted graffiti on the walls. They poured cans of paint on the seats. They—"

"I'll be right there," Nick cut in, as he slammed down the receiver.

■ ■ ■

Surveying the damage, Nick felt sick. So many people had worked so hard to clean up the place! Why would anyone want to sabotage their work?

"This is just *great!* Now Gloria will remind

everybody that this is a bad luck play," Nick muttered to himself.

The next day, Nick met with the cast and crew. He was surprised at Gloria's reaction. She looked sad when she heard the bad news. "I'm so sorry about this, Nick," she said sympathetically. "We never had any vandalism five years ago."

Luckily, the volunteers refused to give up. "So we have to start over," one man said stubbornly. "So be it. I'm not about to let a bunch of punks close down the theater. Somebody hand me a paintbrush!"

"Mr. Finney, phone call!" a voice shouted from backstage.

Nick sighed as he hurried out to take the call.

■ ■ ■

As he made his way to the stage manager's office, Nick thought about everything that had happened. The damage was being repaired. The volunteers were already tearing down the burned section of the theater. "The vandals set us back," Nick thought, "but they couldn't stop us!"

Nick picked up the receiver and said hello. The voice on the other end sounded hysterical. It was Joe's wife, calling from the Cold Forks hospital.

"Joe's been in a terrible accident!" Mrs. Collier cried. "You'll have to cancel rehearsal tonight."

Nick froze. "Oh, no! How badly is he hurt?" Nick asked. "Tell me what happened!"

Mrs. Collier was rather vague. Nick thought she might be in shock. "Shall I come to the hospital?" he asked.

"No!" she exclaimed. "But you'll have to cancel rehearsal for a couple of weeks. By then, Joe should be better."

Nick knew he couldn't do that. They'd just have to work around the missing man. He sent Joe his best wishes and hung up.

"First vandalism, and then an auto accident," Nick thought. "Could be *Macbeth* really is a bad luck play!"

Nick hurried back to give everyone the

bad news. As he walked onstage, he saw that Gloria was rehearsing some of her character's most famous lines. In the sleepwalking scene, Lady Macbeth is feeling enormous guilt about her part in the king's murder. She imagines that her hands are permanently stained with the king's blood.

"Out, damned spot. Out, I say!" She rubbed her hands furiously, as if washing them. *"Here's the smell of the blood still. All the perfumes of Arabia will not sweeten this little hand."*

Suddenly there was a loud cracking sound. Nick looked up. A heavy piece of scenery was about to topple over! Nick heard several people cry out. Without thinking, he dove forward.

He knocked Gloria to one side, just as the backdrop crashed to the stage. Gloria wasn't hurt, but Nick felt a sharp pain shoot through his leg.

In the hospital emergency room, the doctor had good news for Nick.

"You'll be black and blue for a while," the

doctor said with a smile. "You don't plan to run a marathon, I hope."

Nick rolled his eyes. "Come on, Doc, what about the play? Can I still direct?"

The doctor nodded. "Nothing's broken, Nick. You can direct as long as you're sitting down. But you're going to be limping for a while."

Nick was relieved. "If I have to, I'll direct it standing on my head!" he said.

When he got back to the theater, Nick found most of the cast and crew taking a lunch break. Harry and Steve had finished eating. They were onstage rehearsing a sword fight.

The banker raised his sword threateningly. *"Lay on, Macduff!"* he roared. *"And damned be him that first cries, 'Hold! Enough!'"*

Then the blade of Harry's sword broke loose from the hilt and flew through the air! Nick gasped in horror as the edge of the blade sliced Steve's cheek. Steve cried out in pain and clapped his hand over the wound. Blood oozed out from between his fingers.

Gloria ran to Steve. "Someone call 911!" she called out. "Tell them we've had another accident."

Nick examined the two pieces of the broken sword. Someone had tampered with it! The "accident" had been anything but accidental.

■ ■ ■

"They have tied me to the stake; I cannot fly, but bear-like, I must fight the course."

The line from *Macbeth* kept running around in Nick's head. He felt as if all the bad-luck events of the last few days had tied his hands. But he couldn't bring himself to cancel the production. Too many townspeople were counting on it.

"This has nothing to do with superstition," Nick thought. "Real people vandalized the theater and tampered with Harry's sword. If I'm right, that piece of scenery was tampered with, too."

Nick went to talk to the set designer. Together they checked the supports that held the heavy backdrop in place. Sure enough, someone had sawed through one of the wooden clamps to weaken it.

"I don't get it." The set designer shook his head. "This is the same kind of stuff that happened five years ago. It makes you wonder what's coming next!"

Nick decided it was time he learned more about what had happened five years earlier. Maybe he'd find a clue about what was going on now.

■ ■ ■

Nick headed for the town library. He looked at back issues of the *Cold Forks Chronicle* on microfilm. He read every issue from five years ago.

It wasn't long before he found a news story about the formation of the little theater group. Then he came across an article announcing tryouts for *Macbeth.* A few weeks later, there were stories about some of the accidents that were happening to members of the cast.

The actor playing *Macbeth* had fallen off the stage and broken an ankle. A stagehand had nearly been electrocuted while the stage lights were being set up. One of the actors had narrowly missed being crushed by a piece of scenery.

"Just like now," Nick thought. He shivered and caught his breath. Then he heard a voice.

"It's too dangerous!"

Nick froze. He recognized that voice. He peered through the bookshelves. Gloria Valdez was standing on the other side. She had her back to Nick as she talked on her cell phone.

"He's going to get suspicious," she hissed. "I tell you, we need to back off!"

She listened a moment longer, then groaned in frustration. Apparently, the person on the other end of the line had hung up on her. Nick was afraid she'd see him, but Gloria was too angry to notice anything. Heading for the front door, she stormed out of sight.

Nick wondered what Gloria had been doing in the library. Then he realized that she'd had a good view of the table where he'd been sitting. Had she followed him there? Had she seen him reading back issues of the newspaper?

Who had she been talking to? A little voice told Nick that this had nothing to do with her businesses. "But maybe a lot to do with *Macbeth,*" Nick thought.

He was sure the answer must lie in the past. Nick went back to his table and started reading again. Before long, he stumbled across the article about the fire. It had made the front page.

Then a shorter piece on the same page caught his eye. *Downtown Bank Branch Robbed,* the headline announced.

As Nick read the article, the pieces started to fall into place. Now he was almost certain that he had the answers he'd been looking for. But he needed *proof.* "There's only one way to find out if I'm right," he thought.

Nick pulled out his cell phone and punched in a number.

■ ■ ■

A few hours later, Nick, the police chief, and several other cops were hunkered down inside the theater. "Are you sure you're right about this?" the chief whispered.

"I hope so," Nick muttered. He wondered what time it was. If something didn't happen pretty soon, he was going to feel mighty foolish.

Suddenly the chief's two-way radio spat a burst of static. "They're at the front door," the lookout warned.

The chief turned off his radio and signaled everyone to be quiet. Moments later, Nick saw flashlight beams cut through the darkness. He heard hoarse whispers. Several people climbed up onto the stage and tiptoed by them. The stage was pitch black. Nick and the cops could only guess what was happening by the sounds the intruders made.

Suddenly, they heard someone cry out, *"I have it!"*

At that moment, Nick flipped a switch and brought the lights up. The chief and the other cops dashed to the burned-out prop room. Bad leg or not, Nick was right behind them.

Gloria, Joe, and Harry were caught in the lights. Harry was holding a stained canvas bag. Joe and Gloria were standing there open-mouthed, staring at the cops in horror.

One of the cops snatched the canvas bag from Harry and peered inside. "This is the money from the robbery, Chief!"

■ ■ ■

"W*hat's done cannot be undone!"*

Nick grinned. When he saw the puzzled look on the chief's face, he explained. "That line is from *Macbeth*. Right now it seems very appropriate."

"Huh? What does *Macbeth* have to do with the bank being robbed five years ago?" the chief asked.

"Gloria, Joe, and Harry talked the little

theater group into putting on *Macbeth* five years ago," Nick explained. "They'd already planned to rob the bank next to the theater. That's why they chose *Macbeth*—because of the play's reputation for bad luck. It wasn't hard for them to set up all the accidents along the way. That made the fire look like just one more disaster!"

Nick leaned back in his chair. "While everyone was watching the theater burn, these three fine citizens robbed the bank. Later, they hid the money in the burned-out prop room. That section of the theater was roped off because it was so unsafe. No one would dare to go in there. I checked out the statute of limitations on grand theft. This greedy little gang had to wait only a little while longer. Then all that money would have been theirs!"

■ ■ ■

The police chief whistled in amazement. "But then you came along," he said with a knowing look. "And you wanted to direct *Macbeth!*"

Nick nodded. "First, they tried to talk me out of it. When that failed, they staged more accidents to set us back. Remember Joe's car accident? He wasn't hurt nearly as badly as he let on."

The chief handed Nick a cup of coffee. "How did you bait the trap?"

"Last night, I phoned Gloria to tell her that rehearsals were canceled for a few days," Nick said, stirring his coffee. "I said the volunteers were going to tear down the burned-out part of the theater right away. That put the pressure on. She knew they had to get the money out immediately. As you see, she didn't waste any time calling Joe and Harry."

"So what now? Are you going to cancel the production?" the chief asked.

Nick shook his head. "No way! I'll have to recast those three parts, of course. And that will mean more rehearsals. But there's no way we'll let the community down!"

Nick smiled widely. "After all, as Mr. Shakespeare said, '*The play's the thing.*'"

After-Reading Wrap-Up

1. What would have happened if Nick had been someone who gave up easily?
2. Outline the book's plot in three or four sentences. In the first sentence, write about the story's unsolved mystery. In the following sentences, tell how the mystery was finally worked out.
3. At one point, Nick compared himself to a tied-up bear. Why did he feel this way?
4. The Bad Luck Play refers to two things. What were they?
5. Nick described Macbeth as "filled with greed, betrayal, murder, ghosts—". Describe something you've read or watched recently that had one or more of these themes.
6. Nick learns about the robbery through hard thinking and research. But he also had a lucky break. What was it?